Show Stopper

Written by Christine Peymani

Bath · New York · Singapore · Hong Kong · Cologne · Delhi · Melbourne

First published by Parragon in 2008
Parragon
Queen Street House
4 Queen Street
Bath BA1 1HE, UK

ISBN 978-1-4075-2048-3

Printed in the UK

"So you see, unless we make some big changes fast, polar bears will be extinct in less than 50 years!" Mrs Whitley, the Stilesville High earth science teacher, told her class, pointing to the chart on her overhead projector.

"What?" Yasmin cried, leaping up from the table where she sat with her best friend Cloe. "But I love polar bears! They're, like, my favourite Arctic animal!"

"Yasmin!" Cloe hissed, tugging at her friend's arm.

Yasmin glanced around and realized that everyone in the classroom was staring at her. She sat back down quickly, her cheeks burning with embarrassment.

"Sorry, Mrs Whitley," she muttered.

"No need to apologize!" Mrs Whitley replied. "It's natural to be upset about the destruction of our environment. And it's not just the polar bears that are in trouble. Lots of other species are facing extinction due to global warming, too."

"So what can we do?" Yasmin asked, before realizing that once again, she had spoken up without raising her hand. She clapped her hand over her mouth and sheepishly stuck her other hand in the air.

"It's okay, Yasmin," her teacher said, smiling. "That's a very good question." Mrs Whitley placed another sheet on the overhead projector, showing the class a list of tips for counteracting global warming. "You can use less energy at home, recycle, plant trees, buy locally and use public transportation more often."

"That doesn't sound too hard," Cloe chimed in. "Is that really enough to save the world?"

"Sure it is, if everyone does it," Mrs Whitley replied.

"Well then, we've just got to make sure they do!" Yasmin exclaimed.

She wanted to ask a lot more questions, but just then, the bell rang.

"Remember, bring in your projects on an environmental issue next time," Mrs Whitley

called after her students as they gathered up their bags and notebooks and hurried out of the classroom. "We'll resume talking about these environmental issues tomorrow."

Yasmin couldn't stop talking about that day's class.

"The environment's really in trouble!" she told Cloe as they headed for the cafeteria together. "There's got to be something we can do!"

"But what?" Cloe asked. "I mean, it seems like a pretty huge problem."

"I don't know," Yasmin admitted. She spotted their best friends Jade and Sasha, who were already sitting at their favourite table, and added, "But I bet together, we can figure it out!"

The girls pulled up chairs and Yasmin was about to launch into an explanation of

what she and Cloe had learned in their earth science class, but before she could say a word, Sasha burst out with her own news.

"I've got big plans for this summer," she announced. "The Starz are going on tour!"

The Starz was the name of the girls' latest musical group, and since Sasha wanted to be a music producer one day, she was always on the lookout for ways to promote their band.

"We were invited to do a show in San Francisco, and another in Washington, D.C.," she explained. "So I figured we might as well add some other cities and make it a cross-country tour. What do you think?"

"That sounds amazing!" Jade exclaimed. "I love exploring new parts of the country!"

But Yasmin bit her lip, looking unsure.

"What's wrong, Yas?" Sasha asked her worriedly. She hoped Yasmin wasn't tired of

the group – Yasmin was the best singer in the group, and there was no way they could go on tour without her!

"Well, it's just–" she glanced over at Cloe for support, and Cloe gave her an encouraging smile. "I was planning to save the earth this summer!"

"Oh, wow!" Jade cried. "But how, exactly?"

"Well, that's what I'm not sure about," Yasmin admitted. "Mrs Whitley was telling us today about how serious global warming is, and I just feel like there has to be something we can do to help."

"Well, at least you don't

think small!" Sasha teased her friend.

"Yeah, but I have no clue what to do," Yasmin admitted with a sigh. "I mean, it's such a huge problem. What can *we* do?"

"Anything we put our minds to!" Cloe squealed, leaping out of her chair and knocking over her bottled water in her excitement.

"That's right," Jade agreed with a smile, helping Cloe mop up the water she had splattered across the table.

As her friends settled back into their seats, Sasha gazed thoughtfully across the lunchroom at the baking sale table the speech team had set up.

"Sash?" Yasmin asked, following her friend's gaze. "I know those cupcakes look totally yummy, but I need you to focus for a minute here!"

"I *am* focused," Sasha protested. "In fact, I just came up with an awesome plan!"

"That's our Sasha!" Cloe declared proudly. She leaned across the table, grinning. "Come on, tell us!"

"We can go on our concert tour *and* save the world!" Sasha announced.

"But how?" Jade asked.

"We'll turn our concerts into a fundraiser," Sasha explained, "just like the speech team's baking sale."

"Only bigger!" Cloe cried.

"And better!" Jade chimed in.

"We could get some other bands to join us and make it into a fabulous summer festival," Yasmin suggested.

"Awesome idea, Yas!" Sasha agreed. "I'll start calling around to all the bands we know

right after school."

"Then we can raise money *and* awareness for the environment," Yasmin added.

"And have a spectacular summer at the same time!" Cloe cried.

"Now *that's* what I call a perfect plan!" Jade declared, exchanging excited smiles with her friends.

Chapter 2

"Roxxi's in," Sasha announced later that night on the phone to Yasmin. Their friend Roxxi had gone solo after they all hit it big as the Rock Angelz, so of course she was the first one Sasha had called.

"That's awesome!" Yasmin cried. "It'll be so great to see her again!" While Yasmin talked she was busy putting the finishing touches on her earth science class project, positioning charts and graphs and adding sparkles to draw attention to her display.

"I know – she's been on the road so much lately that it's been forever since we got to hang out with her," Sasha agreed. "And she loves the idea of using her music to help the planet."

Yasmin nodded approvingly at her finished

project, then flopped down among the fluffy pile of pillows on her bed with a sigh. "But Sasha, do you really think singing is the best way to save the environment? Shouldn't we, you know, get out there and clean up the beaches or something?"

Sasha flipped through the neatly organized concert tour plans she had spread out on her desk as she listened. "We can do that too. But if it's a publicized stop on our tour, people will pay way more attention, which means we can get more people to help out and get a lot more done than the four of us could do alone."

"That's true ..." Yasmin added with uncertainty, staring up at the ceiling. "But it just feels – I don't know – *silly* to try to fix such big problems with music."

"What are you talking about?" Sasha cried, pushing her chair back from her desk and pacing the room excitedly. "What's more

11

inspirational and influential than music? Why do you think there were all those protest singers in the sixties?"

"Good point . . ." Yasmin began, but Sasha was on a roll.

"It's because songs stick with people! Songs tap into what's most meaningful to people! So if we sing about saving the world . . ."

"We can actually convince people to do it!" Yasmin exclaimed. She grabbed her favourite notebook from her bedside table and started scribbling. "Sasha, you just inspired me to write a song about healing the planet!"

Sasha settled back into her chair, looking very pleased with herself. "That's the spirit, Yas!"

"Can I call you back? I want to get this down while it's fresh in my mind," Yasmin said, still writing furiously.

"Absolutely," Sasha agreed. "I wouldn't want to stand in the way of a true genius!"

The next morning, as soon as Yasmin's three best friends had piled into her car on the way to school, she started singing them her new tune.

"It's really rough," she warned them, before belting out her beautifully written lyrics in her clear, sweet voice.

"Wow, if that's rough, I can't wait to hear polished!" Jade declared, making Yasmin blush.

"Thanks, Jade," Yasmin murmured.

©MGA

"Seriously, that song's a winner!" Sasha added. "We'll have to make that the big showstopper number for the whole tour. Maybe we can even get the other acts to perform it with us!"

"That would be so cool," Jade agreed. "Hey, Yas, what do you call it?"

"Well, I'm not sure yet, but I was thinking of 'Charmed Planet'," Yasmin replied. "What do you think?"

"I think you just found us the name for our tour!" Sasha exclaimed.

"Ooh, yeah," Cloe added. "I can just see us all decked out like sixties folk singers, holding hands and singing Yasmin's new hit song!"

"Love it!" Jade squealed. "I'll start designing our outfits tonight."

"And I'll get to work on the sets!" Cloe exclaimed.

"And I've got a *lot* more phone calls to make if we're going to turn this into the concert event of the summer!" Sasha chimed in.

As the girls grabbed their bags and hopped out of the car, Yasmin gave each of her best friends a huge smile. "Girls, I think we just might pull this off."

"How could you ever doubt it?" Sasha teased, slinging her arm around Yasmin's shoulders. "Don't you know yet that together, we're invincible?"

When Yasmin and Cloe walked into their earth science class that morning, it was already filled with projects on everything from endangered species to global warming, pollution to energy conservation. The girls quickly set up their own projects – Cloe's on the destruction of coral reefs, Yasmin's on

protecting the rainforests – and then eagerly examined all the other projects set up around the room.

"We need something like this for our concert tour," Yasmin declared. "You know, booths where people can really learn about the problems facing our planet, and what they can do to help."

"Awesome idea, Yas!" Cloe agreed. "It'll give it a real festival vibe. I'll start sketching some booth designs tonight."

"What's this about a festival?" Mrs Whitley asked, joining the girls beside an exhibit showing the effects of deforestation.

"Oh, Mrs Whitley, I wanted to tell you," Yasmin began excitedly. "You totally inspired us to help save the planet! So we're putting together a save-the-world concert tour this summer to get the word out!"

"That sounds great, girls," their teacher replied. "Is there anything I can do to help?"

"We'd love to get your input on how to make the tour as environmentally friendly as possible," Yasmin told her.

"And it would be awesome if you could help us figure out what issues to tell people about, since we want the festival to be totally educational," Cloe added.

"I think I could manage that," Mrs Whitley replied with a smile. "I would definitely recommend using all the topics your classmates have covered today!"

"Oh, absolutely," Cloe agreed. The bell rang, indicating the start of class, and Mrs Whitley wove through the tables laden with presentations to take her place at the front of the classroom.

"Well, I want to have each of you present

your projects to the class, but first, I have some exciting news to share!" Mrs Whitley announced. "Your classmates, Cloe and Yasmin, are putting together a concert tour this summer to save the planet."

"Oh, wow!" squealed the girls' friend Kumi from across the room.

"That's so cool of you," their friend Cade added.

"Well, it isn't just us," Yasmin said modestly. "Sasha and Jade are in on it, too."

"I think it's wonderful to see you putting what you've learned in this class into practice," Mrs Whitley announced. "I think we should all try to do the same. So, I'd like each of you to come up with a booth based on your project that can be set up at the girls' festival. Think about including information of course, but also activities to get people interested, and clear explanations of how they can help.

To give you an added incentive to make your display really great, this will count as your final project for this course."

"Thank you so much!" Yasmin exclaimed. "It'll be a huge help to have everyone working on these booths."

"It'll be totally fun to be working on something that the whole country will get to see," their friend Dana added.

"Yeah, and something that can really help change the whole world!" their pal, Bryce, chimed in.

The girls were thrilled to see how pumped up their classmates and teacher were about the idea of their tour. Everyone was chattering about how they could improve their projects to make them utterly eye-catching for the festival – everyone, that is, except for a small, blonde girl named Mira, who Yasmin didn't know very well.

Cloe was too caught up in everyone else's excitement to notice, but Yasmin saw Mira just sitting in the corner, staring glumly at her exhibit on the ozone layer. Yasmin wanted to go and talk to her, and see if she was okay, but she decided it would be awkward since they had hardly ever spoken before. Besides, Cloe was tugging at her arm, trying to show her one project after another and explain her big ideas for making them even better. Soon Yasmin was following her best friend around the room, too caught up in her friend's enthusiasm to remember her concerns about a girl she barely knew.

Chapter 3

That night, the girls decided to have a combination sleepover and planning session at Sasha's house. With school almost over for the summer, they couldn't wait to get started on their awesome new tour!

Once the girls had all found comfy spots to lounge in Sasha's room, Sasha pulled out a chart listing the potential line-up so far. "First of all, The Dragons and The Tiger Stripes are in."

"Omigosh, Sasha, those bands have, like, the cutest lead singers!" Cloe squealed.

"I thought you might appreciate those selections," Sasha replied with a smile.

"How'd you get such big acts on board?" Jade wanted to know.

"You forget, I've got connections!" Sasha said. "Plus, they're with Groove Records just like us, so I got our producer to make the introduction."

"That's fantastic, Sash!" Yasmin cried.

"I also got Sugar Sugar – Roxxi's good friends with them, so that one was easy," Sasha added. "And Byron Powell's new group, The Cosmic Quarks, is joining the tour as well."

Byron was a big-time producer who had helped the girls form their rock band, the Rock Angelz.

22

"Wow, this is gonna be the coolest concert tour ever!" Cloe exclaimed.

"Do you think six acts is enough to make it a really spectacular event?" Sasha asked.

"That sounds perfect," Yasmin assured her friend. "Thank you so much for taking the lead on all of this. But I feel bad that you're doing all the work!"

"Hey, this is the fun part for me," Sasha replied. "I'll book the artists and the venues, and you girls can take over on the rest of the tour. How's that sound?"

"I think that's fair – especially since you're taking on all the hard stuff!" Jade agreed.

"I can't believe this is all coming together so fast!" Yasmin exclaimed.

"So where are we all going on our tour?" Jade wanted to know.

"Since we have so many bands to move

23

around, I figured we shouldn't have *too* many stops," Sasha said. "So we already have Washington, D.C. and San Francisco, and I'm setting up concerts in Atlanta and Phoenix as well. I wanted to make sure we hit cities that we didn't make it to last summer."

"Ooh, that sounds like so much fun!" Cloe cried. "Hey, I heard Austin has an awesome music scene too – what would you think about doing a show there?"

"Great idea, Cloe," Sasha agreed. "I'll work on booking that in the morning."

"Five stops across the country," Jade mused. "Yep, I think that'll do for getting the word out about the environment!"

"Those sound like really fun cities," Yasmin chimed in. "And I've never been to any of them, so I'm sure we'll have a fabulous time exploring them all."

"Of course we will!" Sasha replied. "So,

Cloe and Jade, do you have any designs to share with us yet?"

"Well, we were brainstorming in art class today, and I think we've come up with a spectacular theme," Jade announced.

"We were thinking about Yasmin's song, and the title made us think of good-luck charms," Cloe explained.

"Plus we were thinking about capturing that sort of hippie vibe with this festival, so here's what we came up with," Jade added, flipping open her sketchpad.

Cloe pulled her sketchpad out as well, and Sasha and Yasmin peered eagerly at the pages.

©MGA

Jade had sketched flared trousers and bell-sleeved peasant blouses, short patterned dresses and tall wedges, all with cute embroidery details like peace signs, hearts and flowers.

"I think these are the perfect outfits for changing the world!" said Jade.

"Totally!" Sasha agreed.

Cloe had designed an elaborate logo for the show, with 'Charmed Planet' at the centre and good-luck symbols like ladybirds, lucky stars, horseshoes and four-leaf clovers in bright colours all around it.

"I thought the sets could incorporate some of these fun symbols, along with inspirational words like 'peace' and 'love' splashed across the backdrop," Cloe explained.

"Cloe, this looks so cool," Yasmin declared. "You've totally captured that whole

flower-child spirit, which is exactly right for what we're trying to do!"

"I also thought we could make lucky charms like the ones I drew here, you know, to sell at the festival," Cloe continued. She turned to the next page in her sketchbook to show her friends the designs. "It would be a great way to raise some extra cash, don't you think?"

"Totally," Sasha agreed. "And we can stamp 'Save the World' on the back of each charm as a little reminder of what they're for!"

"You know what, girls?" Yasmin asked. "All this 'luck' talk makes me wonder – do you think we should change our name to the Lucky Starz for this tour?"

"Ooh, Yasmin, I love it!" Cloe exclaimed.

"I'll get the word out to the label and the venues right away," Sasha added.

"I have such a good feeling about this, girls!" Yasmin cried. "I just know we're gonna make a huge difference for the planet!"

Chapter 4

The girls scrambled to finish all their schoolwork for the year while still planning the most fabulous festival of the summer.

"You guys, I'm totally beat," Cloe moaned midway through finals week, slumping into an overstuffed chair beside her friends in the school library. "I can't believe we still have to take all these tests when we're out trying to save the world! We should get, like, extra credit or something."

"We *are* getting extra credit in earth science," Yasmin pointed out. "But it's not like this concert tour is exactly helping us out with our English or maths skills."

"It could!" Cloe insisted.

"How?" Sasha asked.

"I don't know ..." Cloe replied. "But there's gotta be a way!"

"Sasha's the one handling everything, anyway," Jade interjected. "So why are you so worn out, Cloe?"

"Hey!" Cloe protested. "I've been putting in some serious design time, trying to get all the promo materials and sets ready." Suddenly, her blue eyes widened with excitement. "That's it! I should be getting extra credit in art class for all this work!"

"Yeah, good luck convincing Mr Del Rio of that," Jade told her, shaking her head.

"Cloe, you're the best artist in school!" Yasmin added. "I'm sure you've got an A-plus in art already."

"That's true..." Cloe admitted.

"I could be wrong, but I think that's about as high a grade as you can get," Sasha teased.

"I just wish I could apply some of my art grade to these other classes," Cloe sighed. She flicked through the pages of a few of the huge textbooks piled on the table in front of her, then shoved them away. "Girls, I need a study break!"

"But you just got here!" Jade reminded her.

"Okay, then, I need a pre-study break!" Cloe announced, making her friends laugh.

"Would a smoothie do the trick?" Sasha asked.

"Totally!" Cloe agreed.

At their favourite smoothie shop, Smooth Moves, Sasha whipped out her PDA so she could update the girls on their tour plans.

"So we've got a two-week, five-city tour," Sasha began. "And I've set up some cool community service projects for us and the other bands along the way."

"That's awesome, Sasha," Yasmin declared. "Where'd you find time for all that?" She shot a pointed look at Cloe, but Cloe just shrugged.

"Hey, we can't all be super-women like Sasha," Cloe replied.

"You wouldn't believe how much more you can get done when you get organized," Sasha informed her friends, tapping away on her PDA.

"Yeah, but that's what we have you for," Jade pointed out.

"Okay, I have a question," Cloe declared, before taking a long sip of her smoothie. "Isn't driving cross-country, like, bad for the environment?"

"I talked to Mrs Whitley about that," Yasmin said, "so we're renting hybrid tour vans that use less fuel and put out fewer pollutants."

"Great idea, Yas!" Jade cried.

"There are also these things called carbon offsets we can buy to make up for the fuel we do use," Yasmin added.

"A carbon what?" Cloe asked.

"It's basically donating money to support projects like replanting forests and building renewable energy facilities," Yasmin explained.

"That's really cool," Sasha said. "I've never heard of that!"

"Yeah, I think it's a new thing," Yasmin replied with a shrug. "So Groove Records agreed to cover it to help our tour go green."

33

"Oh yeah, speaking of going green, we're booked into venues that are using electricity from renewable resources, like wind, water and sun," Sasha chimed in.

"I wanted to see if we could have all the promotional materials printed on recycled paper, too," Jade added.

"Jade, you're a genius!" Sasha cried. "Girls, this is gonna be the greenest concert tour ever!"

"Yeah, and also the *greatest!*" Cloe declared.

The four friends raised their smoothies in a toast before dissolving in giggles.

The girls survived the next few days of classes, and then it was time to hit the road.

"I can't believe I never knew what a huge impact taking a road trip would have on the environment," Cloe told her friends in the

back of their tour van.

"I know, it's crazy, isn't it?" Yasmin asked. "And a lot of other people don't know it, either. Which is why this tour is so important!"

"Exactly!" Sasha agreed from the front seat.

Sasha was a take-charge kind of girl, so she had offered to drive for the first leg of their trip.

"I can't wait to meet the other groups!" Jade added, turning around in the seat next to Sasha so she could see her friends in the back. "They must be really cool people to join us on supporting such an important cause, don't you think?"

"Definitely," Cloe agreed. "Which is why I think those boy-bands' lead singers are totally crushworthy!"

"Um, Cloe, didn't you have huge crushes on both of them *before* they signed on for this tour?" Sasha pointed out.

"Well, yeah, but now I like them both even more!" Cloe replied.

"We'll meet them this afternoon," Sasha replied. "Then you can see what you really think of them."

"I'm sure they'll be wonderful," Cloe insisted.

Her friends just grinned at her. Cloe was always developing huge crushes, so the girls had trouble taking Cloe's current obsession too seriously.

Chapter 5

The girls spent the hours of driving to San Francisco chatting and practising their new songs.

When they crossed the Golden Gate Bridge into the winding streets of San Francisco, Jade gasped at the view. "What an incredible city! I think I'm gonna like it here."

They checked into the hotel suite they were sharing to get ready to meet the other artists.

"Ooh, this is *nice!*" Cloe sighed, flopping onto the cushy bed she had claimed for herself. "Who knew being eco-friendly could also be so chic?"

They were staying in the greenest hotel in the country, the Viewpoint Hotel, where the

bedding and towels were all made of organic cotton, the electricity came from solar panels and wind power, and all the rooms were set up for recycling and water conservation.

"Why shouldn't they go hand-in-hand?" Sasha asked. "I mean, it's definitely hip and modern to care about the environment."

"Good point," Cloe agreed, snuggling deeper into the fluffy pillows on her bed.

"Don't get too comfortable!" Yasmin told her friend. "We're meeting the other bands in half an hour – don't you want to dress to impress?"

"Hey, are you trying to say I don't look good already?" Cloe protested. She sat up in bed and playfully threw a cushion at Yasmin.

"Of course not!" Yasmin replied. "But we *have* been cooped up in a van together all day. I wouldn't say any of us exactly look

our best right now!"

"Yeah, I'd forgotten how icky road trips make me feel," Jade added. "I'm just glad to have a hot shower waiting for me here."

"Come on girls, we better get a move on – we can't be late for our own meeting!" Sasha pointed out.

Each of the girls bustled into one of the four bathrooms in their suite and hurried to get ready. After a quick shower, they each emerged in one of the outfits Jade had put together for the tour. They wore flared jeans and peasant blouses with charm

bracelets for a casual yet totally chic look.

"I hope those other bands can keep up with our fashion forwardness," Jade said, striking a pose in front of the dressing-table mirror in the suite's main room.

"Well, if not, you can always give them a makeover!" Yasmin suggested.

Jade looked thoughtful. "Yeah, I guess I could manage that."

"For sure," Sasha agreed. She glanced at her watch, and gasped, "Girls, we've gotta get down to the lounge – we don't want to keep our co-stars waiting!"

When the girls reached the hotel's lounge, it was already crowded with members of the other bands. First they spotted Roxxi, perched on the edge of a chair, and rushed over to give her a hug. "Girl, it's been too long!" Sasha squealed.

"I know – but this is the perfect occasion for a reunion tour, don't you think?" Roxxi replied. The girls all nodded in agreement.

"Hey, I want you to meet my friends Serena and Shawna," Roxxi added, motioning two sweet-looking girls standing nearby over to them. "Together, they're the group Sugar Sugar!"

"I *love* your music," Jade gushed, shaking the girls' hands.

"And we love yours," Serena replied with a smile.

"And we love this amazing tour you've put together," Shawna added. "Thanks so much for inviting us along."

"Hey, are these the famous Lucky Starz?" asked a young man with curly blonde hair, strolling over to join them.

"Omigosh, you're Cody, lead singer of

The Dragons!" Cloe gasped. "I am, like, your biggest fan!"

"And you're Cloe," Cody said, grinning. "I'm a pretty big fan of yours, too."

Cloe was so excited that she couldn't say another word, so Sasha stepped forward and introduced herself to the other two members of Cody's band, Riley and Brady.

"You must be The Tiger Stripes," Cloe said, finally recovering her voice and turning to the

©MGA

four other guys who had gathered nearby.

"We sure are," a tall, skinny guy replied. "I'm Tristan, and these guys here are Ashton, Parker and Carter." He smiled at Cloe, but then turned to Yasmin, who was hanging back a little, feeling shy. "And you must be Yasmin. I hear all this was originally your idea."

"Oh, I don't know, we kind of all came up with it together–" Yasmin began, but Jade stopped her.

"She's just being modest," Jade announced. "This was totally Yasmin's brainchild. The rest of us just helped."

"Hey, hope we didn't miss the party," said a golden-haired girl, striding into the room with a guy and another girl behind her.

"Nope – you're right on time," Sasha replied. "I take it you're The Cosmic Quarks?"

"That's us," the girl said. "I'm Brooke, and

these are my band mates, Skylar and Jack."

"It's great to meet you," Yasmin said, shrugging off her shyness and shaking hands with the new arrivals.

"We just wanted to make sure we all had a chance to get to know each other before we start sharing a stage," Sasha announced, getting the group's attention. "And we thought we should practise our new song, "Charmed Planet", which we'll all perform together at the end of each show."

"That's a great song, Yasmin," Tristan declared. "I'm totally pumped to perform it."

"Oh – thanks," Yasmin replied, her eyes downcast.

With her gaze lowered, she didn't notice Cloe shooting an annoyed look at her. Cloe didn't like her friend hogging all of Tristan's attention, even though her other crush, Cody,

had settled onto the sofa right beside her.

Jade closed the doors to the lounge, and the groups ran through the song together. After a couple of tries, their unique sounds blended into a harmonious chorus.

"This is gonna be a killer concert!" Cody announced, and the others couldn't help but agree.

Chapter 6

That night, the amphitheatre was jam-packed. The Lucky Starz watched the other bands go on, and were thrilled to see their awesome shows. Sugar Sugar was totally upbeat and high-energy, The Cosmic Quarks had an edgy rock sound, The Tiger Stripes were totally chilled, and The Dragons blew the audience away with their high-powered ballads. And, of course, Roxxi's solo performance brought down the house.

When it was their turn onstage, the girls twirled under the flashing, low-energy lights, and their singing had never sounded better. The patterned mini-dresses Jade had designed for their tour debut fluttered around them as they danced, the bright colours of the fabrics

flashing in the spotlights. Each girl wore a lucky charm bracelet that Cloe had made, and the tiny charms jingled softly as they moved to the music.

All evening long, people explored the booths set up around the edges of the amphitheatre, signing up for volunteer events and learning about how they could help the environment. Everyone was so excited and eager to help, and they went completely wild when the bands all took the stage together and sang "Charmed Planet".

Backstage, the groups chattered happily, thrilled at how perfectly the show had gone.

"That was probably the best concert we've ever given!" Brooke declared.

"Us too!" Riley chimed in, smiling at her.

"The energy was incredible," Cloe agreed. "I'm so glad we decided to do this!"

"I know, I really think we're making a difference," Yasmin told the others.

"Definitely," Sasha replied. "But if we want to keep making a difference, I think we'd all better get some rest. Tomorrow we're doing a coastal clean-up, and then we hit the road again for our concert in Phoenix."

As they were packing up, Yasmin spotted a familiar-looking blonde girl helping out backstage, but she was so tired from her busy day that by the next second, she had forgotten about the girl completely. Yasmin grabbed her guitar and piled into the tour van with her friends, not noticing the girl lurking outside, watching them go.

The bands all met up on the beach early the next morning, dressed in shorts and T-shirts bearing Cloe's Charmed Planet logo.

"I can't believe people would mess up a beautiful beach like this," Jade complained, staring at the rubbish scattered on the sand.

"Come on, girls, let's makeover this beach!" Cloe cried.

"Check it out, here come the camera crews," Sasha said. "Now is our chance to show people what happens when they're careless with their natural resources."

The girls and their new friends were excited to see how many people had come out to join their volunteer efforts. The beach was crowded with people, many of them wearing

©MGA

their own Charmed Planet T-shirts, and all of them eager to help clean up the beach.

"The Charmed Planet Tour is off to a spectacular start, with a sold-out kick off concert last night, followed by this morning's coastal clean-up, with the tour's stars leading by example and getting their hands dirty with the crowd," said a young reporter as the camera rolled. "And it was all started by these four girls standing beside me."

She motioned Cloe, Jade, Sasha and Yasmin over to her.

"What gave you the idea for this festival, girls?" the reporter asked.

"We were learning about the environment in school, and we just wanted to do something to help," Yasmin explained.

"There you have it – this massive effort to save the planet started in a high-school classroom," the reporter declared, smiling at

the camera. "Now that's what I call education at its finest!"

Soon, other reporters surrounded the four girls, along with the other bands. They were so busy with all the interviews that they hardly had time to do any of the actual cleaning they had come to do.

"I feel like we didn't really help out today," Yasmin complained when the event was over and they were on their way to their next show.

"Of course we did!" Sasha told her. "We got the word out about saving the world. And isn't that really what this tour is all about?"

"That's true . . ." Yasmin admitted, but she couldn't help feeling guilty for basking in the spotlight instead of taking a hands-on role in cleaning up the planet. She promised herself she would really pitch in on their next service project, no matter how many reporters were pushing for an interview.

The Charmed Planet convoy of tour vans wound through the desert that surrounded Phoenix.

Suddenly, Cloe noticed a cloud of smoke billowing around The Dragons' van behind them, and pulled over to the side of the road. The other vans followed, and everyone piled out into the searing desert sun to see find out what was wrong.

"It just stopped running," Brady explained. "I don't know what happened."

"It's so weird," Cody added. "We just had that van checked out this morning, since we knew we had such a long drive ahead of us. The mechanic said it was fine."

"Well, you can ride with us, if you want," Cloe offered.

"I could live with that," Cody agreed.

While one of the equipment managers

dealt with the broken-down van, The Dragons divided up into the other vans, and the groups continued toward Phoenix.

They arrived at their hotel late that night, and all went straight to their rooms to crash. But the next morning, when they met up for breakfast, the girls noticed that the members of The Cosmic Quarks were missing.

"Maybe they just overslept," Jade suggested. "I know *I'd* like to still be sleeping!"

"Yeah, but we have a volunteer event this morning," Sasha pointed out. "So we need to figure out where Brooke, Skylar and Jack are so we can get over there!"

"I'll go and check on them," Yasmin offered. She took the lift up to the floor where all of them were staying, and knocked on Brooke and Skylar's door.

"Who is it?" asked a weak-sounding voice from inside.

"It's Yasmin – can I come in?" Yasmin asked.

After a moment, Brooke slowly pulled open the door and let Yasmin in. She looked very different from the polished-looking girl they had met a couple of days earlier, with her face pasty and her hair a tangled mess.

"Are you all right?" Yasmin wanted to know.

"I don't think so," Brooke replied in a raspy voice. "And whatever it is, Skylar and Jack have it too."

"I called Jack's room to see if he could get us some chamomile tea, but he was just as sick as we are," Skylar added from her bed.

"What happened to you guys?" Yasmin peered at the girls with concern.

"I don't know . . . we ordered room service when we got in, and, ever since then, we've

54

been sick," Skylar told her.

"Do you think there was something wrong with the food?" Yasmin wondered.

"Maybe . . . I mean, it tasted okay, but I don't know what else it could be," Skylar said.

"I'm so sorry, but I really don't think we can continue on the tour," Brooke murmured, settling back onto her bed. "I just don't think we'll be up to it anytime soon."

"I totally understand," Yasmin assured her. "You've got to take care of yourself. I'll go and get the hotel nurse, and then we'll get you guys back home."

"Thanks, Yasmin," Brooke sighed, her voice barely above a whisper.

Yasmin slipped out of the room, sent up the nurse, and then told the others what had happened.

"Ew, I'm glad I didn't get any room service

here," Shawna declared. "It's gotta be food poisoning."

"That's awful!" Cloe cried. "I hope they'll be okay."

"Me too," Sasha agreed. "And I hope our tour will be okay, too. They're a hot new band – they were a pretty big attraction."

"Sasha!" Yasmin protested. "The important thing right now is to make sure they're okay."

"Of course!" Sasha exclaimed. "It's just bad timing, that's all."

"That's an understatement," Jade replied, shaking her head.

Chapter 7

"You don't think we're being sabotaged, do you?" Cody asked the girls in the van on the way to their next project. "Some of the other guys were saying that between the breakdown and the food poisoning, maybe someone's out to get us. Like, some anti-environment group or something."

"I don't know about that," Sasha replied. "It seems more like bad luck to me."

"Yeah, and after how lucky we've been with everything leading up to this tour, I think we're about due for a couple of things to go wrong," Jade added.

"That's true . . ." Cody admitted. "So you don't think we should be worried?"

"No way!" Cloe told him. "And if someone *is* trying to mess up our tour, don't worry – we'll take care of them!"

"Cloe's really tough," Jade explained to Cody with a laugh.

"I *am*!" Cloe protested, and the others joined in Jade's laughter.

They pulled up at Desert State University, where a team of conservationists and landscape designers was

58

waiting for them.

"Because we live in the desert here in Phoenix, water is a very precious resource for us," one of the water conservation experts explained.

"We've teamed up with these designers to create desert-friendly landscapes that make more sense for our climate than lush green lawns," another of the scientists chimed in.

"Today you'll be helping us give the campus a new look," one of the landscape designers added. "We'd love to get your input on our design plans, and then we'll all work together to plant cacti and arrange rock gardens."

"Wow, I've never done a garden makeover before," Jade said, "but I'm totally ready to give it a try!"

Sasha and Yasmin looked excited too, but

Cloe hung back, looking worried.

"What's the matter, Cloe?" Yasmin murmured, pulling her friend aside.

"Don't you think planting cacti is a little *dangerous?*" Cloe asked. "I mean, what if they prick us or something?"

"I'm sure the people running this project know their way around a cactus," Yasmin pointed out. "They do redesigns like this all the time!"

"Yeah, but with the bad luck we've been having lately, I just bet something will go wrong," Cloe insisted.

"Okay, tell you what – you stick to sprucing up the rock gardens, and I'll tackle the cacti," Yasmin offered.

Cloe finally gave Yasmin a grin. "I don't think *tackling* a cactus would actually be a good idea."

"Huh," Yasmin replied with a laugh. "I guess you've got a point there."

"No, the *cacti* have points!" Cloe declared.

"Uh-oh, I think the desert heat's getting to Cloe!" Yasmin announced as she led Cloe back over to join the group.

The band members teamed up with the scientists and designers to revamp gardens all over the campus. Cloe found herself paired up with Cody, and she couldn't have been happier.

"I've never done much gardening," he admitted as he dug a hole to plant a tall saguaro cactus.

"Oh, me neither!" Cloe exclaimed. "But it looks like you're doing a great job!"

He paused in his digging and gave her a sweet, crooked smile. "Thanks, Cloe. You're not doing too bad, yourself."

Cloe blushed, turning her attention to the rock bed she was arranging into a swirly pattern so she wouldn't have to meet Cody's gaze.

On the other side of campus, Yasmin worked with Tristan to work out an eye-catching design for a batch of succulents they were planting by the school's front entrance.

"What about this?" Yasmin suggested, scribbling a quick sketch on the little notebook she always carried for jotting down ideas.

"Looks awesome to me!" Tristan declared. The landscape designer strolled over to check out their plan, and nodded in approval.

"You are a girl of many talents, Yasmin," Tristan declared. "I mean, you write, you sing, you design cool gardens . . . is there anything you can't do?"

"Um, I'm not that great at dodge ball," Yasmin offered, trying to play off the

compliment but unable to hide her smile.

"You know, I think that's one skill you can probably get by without," Tristan told her.

Yasmin laughed, but quickly forced herself to focus on laying out the plants in the pattern she had suggested. She was determined not to flirt with Tristan until she was absolutely sure that Cloe was into Cody instead, but Tristan wasn't making it easy.

When she spotted Sasha working side by side with Shawna in the next garden, Yasmin dropped her spade for a second to go and talk to her friend.

"Now do you feel like you're helping enough?" Sasha asked Yasmin.

"It's definitely a step in the right direction," Yasmin replied. Shielding her eyes from the glare of the sun, she said timidly, "Hey, Sasha, can I talk to you for a sec?"

"You kind of already are," Sasha pointed out.

"Right – I mean, I know – okay, look, I'll just say it," Yasmin stammered. "I think Tristan likes me."

"That's awesome!" Sasha told her. "He seems like a really sweet guy."

"He is," Yasmin agreed. "Which is why *Cloe* likes him too."

"I really wouldn't worry about it," Sasha assured her friend. "Cloe's totally into Cody."

"I don't know ... I don't want to make her mad," Yasmin said.

"Look, if you like Tristan, you should go for it." Sasha waved at Tristan, and Yasmin turned to see him watching them. "I think you better get back over there!"

Yasmin jogged back to her assigned garden to help her new friend.

By the time each team finished redoing their garden, the bands had to rush off to get ready for that night's performance.

"Ugh, I don't think I've ever needed a shower more than I do right now," Cloe complained, tugging at her sweaty, dust-streaked shirt.

"I think we're all in the same boat," Sasha pointed out.

"Good thing we all have our own bathrooms!" Jade added.

"That was really cool though, huh?" Yasmin asked. "I mean, I never thought about it before, but using plants that don't need a lot of water is really smart."

"Yeah, plus those desert gardens are totally hip!" Jade replied. "I'm gonna try to talk my parents into putting one in."

"Good luck with that," Yasmin teased her. Jade's parents had way more traditional taste than Jade did, and her friends doubted that she would be able to talk them into a cutting-edge look for their lawn.

"So you guys know we'll have to perform longer sets tonight, right?" Sasha interrupted. "With The Cosmic Quarks gone, we've all gotta fill in for them."

"Sure thing, Sash," Cloe replied. "You know I don't mind a little extra stage time!"

"I really hope Brooke, Skylar and Jack are okay," Yasmin said worriedly. "They looked horrible this morning!"

"They're on their way home now – I'm sure they'll be fine," Sasha reassured her.

"I just hope nothing else goes wrong," Cloe muttered, staring out of the window at the desert.

Chapter 8

At their concert that night, all of Cloe's carefully designed sets went missing. In their place were signs with slogans like 'Save the Manatees', 'Go Green' and 'Reduce, Reuse, Recycle'.

"Well, it *does* fit with the concert's theme," Jade pointed out.

"Yeah, but it doesn't fit with my vision for this event, *at all!*" Cloe complained. "The sets I designed were totally eye-catching, and these are just so *blah*."

"We'll find the sets you designed," Yasmin promised. "But in the meantime, I think these will have to do."

The four best friends, with the help of the other bands, arranged the signs into a

cool-looking, collage-like backdrop for their performance.

"I guess that'll work," Cloe admitted as they all stood back, admiring their handiwork. "And it certainly gets our message across!"

The audience seemed totally into the event once again, so that helped perk Cloe up. The auditorium was packed, and between acts, huge crowds milled around the booths. Everyone seemed excited to learn about the environment, and to try to help make the world better.

By the time the groups all gathered onstage to sing "Charmed Planet", they were all exhausted but happy. The four remaining bands had held a last-minute rehearsal to figure out a new arrangement for the song with The Cosmic Quarks missing. Sasha had been worried about the last-minute changes, but they had managed to pull it together, and they

all felt good about their new sound.

After the show, the groups met up in their hotel's restaurant for dinner before they went to bed.

"I still think someone's trying to destroy our tour," Cloe declared once they had all grabbed seats at the restaurant's biggest table.

"Why would anyone want to do that?" Serena wondered. "I mean, we're just out there making music. Who could have a problem with that?"

©MGA

"But we're *not* just making music," Yasmin pointed out. "We're trying to make a difference, and there are a lot of people who might have a problem with *that*."

"Why?" Carter asked, his green eyes wide. "I mean, we all have to live on this planet. Why shouldn't we try to protect it?"

"Because there are people who make a lot of money from things like dumping pollutants in the ocean or cutting down forests," Sasha replied. "So I can see why they might not be fans of an event like this."

"You don't really think someone's out to get us, do you?" Roxxi asked.

"No," Sasha admitted. "It's just bad luck. Don't worry, things will start to look up soon."

"I hope you're right," Cloe said grimly, not sounding at all convinced.

When Cloe got an idea, she tended to get

71

completely swept up in it, and it was almost impossible to get her to change her mind. Her friends tried to cheer her up, but Cloe remained convinced that someone was out to get them, and that things would just keep getting worse.

The girls' alarm clocks woke them up bright and early the next morning, and they all stumbled out of bed and wandered around, bleary-eyed, packing up their things for the day's drive.

"I'd forgotten how much being on the road wears me out," Yasmin moaned as she tugged a brush through her long hair.

"I know," Jade agreed. "We aren't even halfway through the tour, and already I'm exhausted!"

"Has anyone seen my charm bracelet?" Cloe

gasped, running through the suite and peering around anxiously. "I put it on my nightstand, and now it's gone!"

"I'm sure it's here somewhere," Sasha told her friend in the soothing voice she used whenever Cloe became frantic. "Let me finish packing, and I'll help you look."

"I've looked everywhere!" Cloe cried. "It's my lucky bracelet, and I can't go on without it, and I just *know* that someone took it to throw off my performance!"

"No one's been in here but us," Yasmin pointed out sensibly. "And none of *us* has any reason to sabotage your singing."

"Of course none of you took it!" Cloe replied. "But someone must have got in here somehow, because it's gone!"

She continued running through the suite, peeking under pillows and rummaging through

73

bags, while her friends exchanged concerned looks.

"I really think this tour is starting to get to Cloe," Jade said. "I'm afraid the stress might be too much for her."

"Nah, you know our Cloe," Sasha assured Jade. "She gets all worked up, but she always calms back down again."

Yasmin made a slow circuit of the suite, and was about to admit that maybe Cloe was right, maybe they were dealing with a thief, when she spotted a glint of metallic blue between Cloe's bed and her nightstand. She ran her hand along the carpet and pulled out a bracelet with hearts, stars and flowers dangling from it.

"Is this it?" Yasmin called, holding the bracelet in the air.

Cloe rushed back into the room, and

74

when she saw what Yasmin was holding, she immediately tackled her best friend with a hug.

"Yasmin, you're a lifesaver!" Cloe gushed. "How did you ever find it?"

"It fell off your nightstand," Yasmin explained. "Probably when you were groping for the snooze button on your alarm this morning."

"Hmm," Cloe replied. She slipped the bracelet back onto her wrist and turned it back and forth, admiring it. She seemed too entranced by her accessories to really pay attention to what Yasmin was saying.

"See, Cloe, there was no reason to freak out," Sasha lectured, joining her friends in Cloe's room.

"Are you kidding?" Cloe demanded. "With everything that's been going wrong on this tour, I couldn't help thinking my charm

bracelet might have been the next target."

"It *is* a cute charm bracelet," Jade pointed out, trying to defuse the rising tension between Sasha and Cloe. "You better keep an eye on it, or I just might snatch it myself!"

"But Jade, you have one just like it!" Cloe told her friend, before noticing the grin on Jade's face. "Oh. You're teasing me."

"That's only because you're tease-worthy, my friend!" Jade replied, and Cloe had to laugh.

"Come on girls, all this drama is slowing us down!" Sasha announced, looking pointedly at her watch. "We've gotta be in the van in ten minutes, and this room is a total disaster!"

"But they can't leave without us, Sasha," Jade pointed out. "We're the stars of the show!"

"Yeah, the *Lucky* Starz," Yasmin teased.

"That's the thing about these group tours," Sasha told her friends. "With all these other cool bands here, they actually *can* put on a show without us."

"They *won't*, though," Jade announced. She slung her embroidered denim tote bag over her shoulder and grabbed her suitcase. "But we should probably get down there anyway."

The girls all headed for the lift, although by the time Cloe dragged all of her luggage in, the door would barely close behind them.

"All right girls, are you ready for some serious driving?" Jade asked as she slipped behind the wheel.

"It's gotta be better than silly driving," Yasmin joked.

"No really, we've got a long day today," Sasha told them.

"Well then, it's a good thing we've got all our best friends here to keep us from getting bored," Cloe pointed out as Jade pulled out of the hotel car park. "With you girls here, the miles will fly by!"

Chapter 9

Fourteen hours later, the tour vans ground to a halt in front of an Austin hotel, and the girls and their new friends burst out of their vehicles.

"Please tell me that was the longest leg of our trip," Cloe said, lugging her piles of suitcases into the hotel lobby.

"Nope," Sasha replied. "The drive from here to Atlanta is just about as long."

"And *why* couldn't we just fly there?" Cloe complained.

"Because aeroplane emissions are really bad for the environment," Yasmin reminded her. "Taking that many flights would do a lot of damage. And we're supposed to be helping the earth with this tour, not hurting it."

"I know, I know," Cloe replied. "I just wish our tour cities were, like, closer together."

"But if they were, it wouldn't exactly be a nationwide tour," Jade pointed out.

"Yeah, well, I've seen enough of the nation," Cloe grumbled.

Her friends shared knowing smiles as Cloe trudged ahead of them. Cloe was always grumpy after a long day, but they could count on her to be cheerful again by the morning, especially since they would get to sleep in for the first time since they had started on this tour.

Sure enough, when Cloe woke up the next morning, she looked totally refreshed and cheerful.

"Mmm, there's nothing like a good night's sleep to make everything seem better," she declared as she strolled into the sunny living

room where Sasha sat sipping a cup of green tea.

"True," Sasha agreed. She had already been up for hours, making calls and sending emails to confirm the remainder of their tour, but she was glad that Cloe had had a chance to recharge.

"Anyone up for breakfast?" Yasmin asked, wandering into the main room.

"Sure!" Cloe agreed. "I'll see if The Dragons want to join us."

"Okay then, I'll call The Tiger Stripes," Yasmin replied, grabbing her mobile phone from her bag.

©MGA

Cloe shot Yasmin an irritated look, but then Cody answered and she turned on the charm.

"Are you awake?" she asked sweetly. "Cool! So grab the guys and meet us in the café!"

Yasmin had headed into her bedroom to call Tristan, and Cloe craned her neck, trying to listen in on her friend's conversation.

When Yasmin reappeared, she couldn't hide her goofy grin.

"So I take it The Tiger Stripes are joining us?" Cloe asked.

"Yep," Yasmin said happily.

Cloe narrowed her eyes at Yasmin, and Jade quickly jumped in to break the tension.

"I just texted Roxxi, and she's meeting us down there with Sugar Sugar," Jade announced.

"Then let's get going, 'cuz those pancakes

are calling!" Sasha declared.

The girls threw on some cute clothes and raced down to the hotel's café, where they found all seven boys already waiting for them.

"Good morning, Yasmin," Tristan called. He patted the chair next to him and added, "I saved you a seat!"

"Can I talk to you for a second?" Cloe asked Yasmin, her teeth clenched.

"Sure," Yasmin agreed.

Sasha and Jade sat down, but kept throwing concerned glances over their shoulders at their friends.

"What is going on with you and Tristan?" Cloe demanded once they were out of earshot.

"Nothing!" Yasmin replied. "I mean, he's been kinda flirty, I guess, but he's just a friend."

"I don't *think* so," Cloe snapped. "Look,

Yasmin, you know I like him, and you're still going after him! That's totally not cool."

"Cloe, you've hardly left Cody's side since we started this tour," Yasmin pointed out. "And now you're gonna tell me you still like Tristan?"

"Well …" Cloe stared down at her strappy sandals, avoiding Yasmin's eyes. "I guess I can see how that's not completely fair."

"I'm not trying to make you jealous," Yasmin said, "and if you want me to quit hanging out with Tristan, I totally will. No way is some guy worth messing with our friendship."

©MGA

Cloe drew in a long breath before answering. "You're right. But you're not the one messing things up – I am. I've just had a crush on Tristan for so long that it was hard for me to see him crushing on you."

"But Cody totally likes you!" Yasmin interrupted.

"And I like him too," Cloe admitted. "I know I was being totally irrational. Can you forgive me?"

"Always!" Yasmin exclaimed, wrapping her best friend in a hug. "Now let's get back there before they beat us to all the food!"

"Everything okay?" Sasha asked as her friends returned to the table.

"Absolutely," Cloe replied. She was happy to see that Sasha was chatting with Carter, The Tiger Stripes' guitarist, while Jade was deep in conversation with The Dragons' drummer, Brady.

"What did we miss?" Roxxi asked, striding into the café with Shawna and Serena following behind her.

Cloe and Yasmin looked at each other and grinned.

"Nothing much," Yasmin said. "Just the first round of orange juice."

After a relaxing breakfast, the bands headed for a local high school, where they were holding an assembly to help other kids learn how to save the environment.

"Even little things like leaving the water running while you brush your teeth can add up to big waste," Yasmin explained, wrapping up her talk on conservation in front of a gymnasium full of fellow teenagers. "Turning it off saves three gallons of water a day! So you see, you really *can* make a difference. Now go out there and do it!"

Yasmin was totally pumped to be sharing the environment-saving tips she had learned from Mrs Whitley and her own research, and her enthusiasm was infectious. When she finished her speech, the students burst into cheers.

Once the crowd had calmed down a little, Yasmin motioned to the rest of the Charmed Planet musicians, and they all ran onstage to perform the tour's theme song a capella. Their voices blended beautifully as they sang Yasmin's heartfelt lyrics, and when the song was over, the audience leapt to their feet, their applause echoing around the gymnasium walls.

"Thank you so much!" Yasmin exclaimed.

"We hope to see you all at our concert tonight!" Sasha added before they all rushed offstage.

"I have to say that was more fun than sweating in the desert heat," Cloe announced

when they were back in their van.

"I really think we made a difference in there, too," Yasmin said, still exhilarated from the students' enthusiastic response.

"Oh, definitely," Sasha agreed. "And after all, that's what this tour's all about!"

Chapter 10

"Wow, this is an amazing turnout," Sasha told the stage manager at that evening's venue. They had passed crowds of people on their way into the amphitheatre, and inside, it was standing-room only.

"Yeah, a little *too* amazing," the stage manager replied. "There's something wrong with the ticketing system, and it looks like the show got oversold. We have lots of very unhappy people out there."

"Isn't there any way we could just fit them all in?" Cloe suggested. "I mean, the more the merrier, right?"

"Not exactly." The stage manager shook her head, her ponytail bobbing emphatically. "There are only so many people this theatre

can hold. Going over that violates fire codes, and we can't do that. We're just going to have to turn a lot of people away."

"Wait!" Sasha protested. "How oversold is it?"

"We sold twice as many tickets as there are seats," the stage manager admitted.

"Okay then, why don't we just do the show twice?" Sasha asked. "We'll be finished with the first show by nine, and then we can launch straight into the second show. Would you guys be up for that?"

The other band members all nodded. "Hey, if it means more money for a good cause, I'll sing all night if I have to," Roxxi declared.

"What do you think?" Yasmin asked, turning eagerly to the stage manager. "Can we make that happen?"

"Sounds good to me," the stage manager

replied. She spoke rapidly into her headset, and moments later, an announcement went out over the venue's loudspeakers, asking everyone who was still waiting to return for a nine o'clock show, and apologizing for the inconvenience.

"You guys are real troupers," the stage manager declared. "You just saved us from a lot of very unhappy customers!"

"Always happy to help," Jade replied with a grin. Turning to her friends, she added, "Well, I guess we'd better get this party started."

"Yeah!" they all cheered, before dashing onstage to greet the crowd.

No one was more surprised than the band members themselves that their second full concert of the night was even better than their first. Their energy continued to build throughout the night, and they all agreed that their final performance of "Charmed Planet" was the best one they had ever given. Plus, the local service projects they were promoting had got more volunteers than they needed, and they had even sold out of the good-luck charm souvenirs Cloe had designed.

"Maybe we should always do double concerts," Parker suggested on their way back to the vans late that night.

"It certainly was a good way to raise more money for the environment," Ashton agreed.

"Yeah, but I have to admit, I'm glad we don't have to do that again," Serena interjected.

"At least we *hope* we don't have to do that again," Cloe pointed out. "After all, we don't know what happened with tonight's ticket sales – so there's no way of knowing whether it'll happen again in Atlanta."

"Oh, come on, what are the odds of something like that going wrong twice in a row?" Jade asked.

"I don't know," Cloe replied darkly. "What are the chances of all the things that have gone wrong on this trip happening in a row, hmm?"

"She's got a point," Roxxi chimed in.

"You guys don't still think someone's trying to ruin our tour, do you?" Tristan asked. "Because if they are, they're doing a pretty bad job of it!"

93

"I bet The Cosmic Quarks wouldn't say they're doing such a bad job," Cloe retorted. "Whoever is behind all this definitely ruined the tour for them."

"Cloe, no one's out to get us," Sasha insisted, but her best friends knew her well enough to see that she wasn't entirely sure about that any more.

They all overslept the next morning, and had to scramble to get on the road in time to make it to Atlanta. After another gruelling day of driving, they had to get up early the next day to plant trees in the city park.

"Are you sure we can't plant trees *later?*" Cloe complained when Sasha woke her the next morning.

"There's no time like the present!" Sasha replied cheerfully.

"Okay, okay," Cloe muttered.

But when they arrived at the park, there were no trees left to be planted.

"Some eager volunteers showed up early this morning and planted them all!" the park director explained. "Sorry to drag you out here for nothing, but we're thrilled to have it all done!"

The reporters who had showed up still snapped some photos of the band members with the trees, but Yasmin was disappointed. "I feel like a fake, posing with these trees when we didn't even plant them."

"Yas, we still *inspired* someone to plant them," Jade pointed out.

"I know I was complaining about getting up early to plant trees," Cloe admitted, "but I still feel bad that someone beat us to it."

"It is kind of weird, isn't it?" Sasha replied.

With a few unexpected hours of free time, the bands decided to check out the city's aquarium.

"It'll be good to see some of the creatures we're helping to save," Yasmin said.

"And we haven't been able to do any sightseeing yet on this tour, so I think it's about time we did!" Cloe added.

The teenagers wandered through the aquarium's sapphire-blue exhibits, admiring the bright-orange fish and milky-white Beluga whales, the silvery rays and

©MGA

translucent, shimmering jellyfish.

"They're incredible," Yasmin murmured to Tristan.

"So are you," he replied, taking her hand. Yasmin couldn't stop smiling, and when Cloe spotted the two of them holding hands, she gave her best friend a thumbs-up. The aquarium had totally taken their minds off the strange things that kept happening on the tour, exactly as they had hoped it would.

They were all feeling good as they drove to the auditorium. Peering out of the window, Yasmin spotted a bunch of sage-green banners reading 'Go Green' fluttering in the breeze.

"Hey, are those ours?" she asked Sasha, but Sasha shook her head.

"But hey, anything eco-friendly's gotta be good for us, right?" Sasha replied.

But when they arrived for the concert, they were hit with another catastrophe. Somehow, ticket sales had got messed up again, but this time, the event was completely undersold. The groups peered out from behind the curtain to see a half-empty auditorium.

"Are people losing interest or something?" Cloe asked worriedly. "Doesn't anybody care about the planet anymore?"

"It's not that. People have been trying to get tickets, but the system claimed it was all sold out," the house manager informed them.

"Well, we've got to fill those seats, fast," Sasha announced. She whipped out her mobile phone and made a few calls.

"Is there a radio somewhere around here?" she asked after she hung up.

"Sure," the house manager replied, looking confused.

She led the Lucky Starz into the main office, while the other bands got ready to perform.

"Sasha, what's going on?" Yasmin wanted to know.

But Sasha just smiled as she flipped on the radio. "This is Mimi at Hot 99.9," announced the DJ, "and let me be the first to tell you that if you aren't at the Charmed Planet concert already, it is time to get over there! They've just released some extra tickets for this one-night-only event, and trust me, you do not want to miss out!"

Sasha turned to another station, and the girls heard a DJ say, "We've got the Lucky Starz, The Dragons, Sugar Sugar, The Tiger Stripes and Roxxi, all together on one stage, all out here trying to save the planet. What could be better than that?"

Sasha continued turning the dial, and on

every station, the announcer was promoting their concert.

"How'd you do that?" Jade asked in amazement.

"Remember that radio internship I did?" Sasha began. Her friends all nodded. "Well, I met a bunch of different DJs, and some of them just happen to work in Atlanta. So I called them and told them what was up, and they called their friends at other stations, and voila, we're about to have ourselves a sold-out concert!"

The house manager had been called away while the girls were listening to the radio, but she rushed back in with a big smile on her face. "You're never going to believe this, but we've got a huge crowd out there – it looks like we're going to be turning people away!"

With that, she bustled off again, and the

girls hurried backstage to prepare for their set.

"Sasha, you are truly amazing," Yasmin announced, giving her friend a hug.

"I do try," Sasha said modestly.

"And boy, are we glad you do!" Jade added as they hurried to tell the other bands the good news.

Chapter 11

"Now do you believe me that someone's behind all this?" Cloe asked the others in the hotel lounge that night.

"Maybe . . ." Sasha admitted. "But who?"

They all stared at each other, but none of them had any ideas. They were still thinking when a crowd of young people in 'Go Green' T-shirts poured into the hotel lobby.

"That was way better than that silly concert tour," a curly-haired girl was saying to a short blonde who Yasmin thought she recognized. "We actually got out there and cleaned up the parks, cleaned up the river and cleaned up the hiking trails, while those guys were just singing about it."

"Hey, isn't that Mira, from our school?" Yasmin asked her friends.

"Oh yeah, we have earth science with her, right?" Cloe replied.

"So what's she doing here?" Sasha wanted to know.

"And what's she doing trashing our concert?" Jade added.

"Looks like we're about to find out," Roxxi declared, as the curly-haired girl strode up to them.

"Well, well, well, look who it is," the girl said. "It's the all-talk, no-action brigade."

"Hey, quit it," Mira hissed, trying to hold her friend back.

"Is there some sort of problem here?" Cody asked, stepping forward.

"Just that you guys *pretend* to care about the planet, while we're out there actually

trying to *do* something about it," the other girl snapped as more 'Go Green' volunteers crowded around behind her.

"But we *have* been doing volunteer work!" Cloe protested. "And we've raised a lot of money for the environment, too!"

"Yeah, I wouldn't exactly call that 'nothing'," Roxxi added.

"Hey Mira, didn't I see you backstage at our show?" Yasmin asked her classmate.

The girl lowered her head and murmured, "Yeah," in a barely audible voice.

"That's right – she sneaked backstage and stole your stupid sets!" the other girl declared.

"Kati, that's enough," Mira told her friend. Turning back to the Lucky Starz, she added, "I didn't steal your sets. I just, you know, *improved* on them a little."

"What are you talking about?" Cloe

104

demanded. "My sets were perfect, and you replaced them with a bunch of glorified bumper stickers! Not cool!"

"Your sets were really pretty," Mira admitted, "but they didn't really say anything about saving the environment. I just thought it would be better to have the message really clearly stated, right there onstage."

"Okay, whoa, we clearly need to talk," Sasha interrupted. "But it's a little bit crowded in here right now. Mira, why don't you come up to our room so we can get the whole story?"

"I'd like that," Mira agreed.

As everyone else cleared out of

the lounge, Mira's friend Kati hung back, but Mira waved her away.

"It's okay," she said. "I've got this."

The five girls headed up to the Lucky Starz' suite and settled into big striped armchairs to talk.

"So have you been on tour with us the entire time?" Jade began once they were all settled.

"Yes," Mira replied.

"So you're the one who's been sabotaging us every step of the way, huh?" Sasha demanded.

"Wait, you didn't poison The Cosmic Quarks, did you?" Cloe gasped. "That was a seriously low blow!"

Mira hung her head, looking miserable, and Yasmin held up her hand to halt her friends' interrogation. "Hang on, you guys. Let

her explain. Mira, what's going on here?"

"I just wanted to help," Mira whispered, her voice so soft that the girls had to lean in to hear her.

"Um, I'm sorry, but how is messing up our concert tour helpful to anyone?" Cloe snapped.

Yasmin shot Cloe a warning look, and Cloe stopped talking abruptly.

"Go on, Mira," Yasmin said encouragingly.

"Well, you know I'm the President of the Stilesville High Earth Club," Mira began.

"I didn't know that!" Sasha cried. "We should totally have got your help in planning this tour!"

"That's exactly what I thought," Mira replied. "I mean, I've been working to raise awareness of environmental issues since I was a kid, and suddenly you girls decide you're into

it and then it's like you're the only ones who ever thought of saving the planet."

"Hey, it wasn't like that!" Cloe protested.

"We didn't mean it like that," Jade interrupted, "but I can see how it might have seemed that way."

"I mean, it's great that you guys are getting the word out," Mira added. "It's just – it's not the way I would've gone about it."

"I can respect that," Sasha told her. "But what I can't respect is you trying to ruin our tour just because you didn't agree with how we chose to try to make a difference."

"That wasn't the reason!" Mira cried. The girls stared at her, and after a moment she admitted, "Well, it sort of was. But I really did want your tour to do well. I just decided to come along and work backstage so I could help nudge it in the right direction, you know?"

"No, we don't know," Cloe snapped.

"But go on, okay?" Yasmin urged. "We're really trying to understand here."

"I didn't do anything to The Cosmic Quarks," Mira continued. "I would never do anything to hurt anyone! I actually think they caught the flu."

"So what *did* you do?" Sasha wanted to know.

"I did cross some wires on The Dragons' van," Mira admitted. "It just seemed wasteful to use five seven-seat vans for 17 people, so I thought I'd take one of them out of commission."

"But Mira, their van broke down in the middle of the desert!" Jade pointed out. "That could've been totally dangerous!"

"Not with a whole caravan of cars behind them," Mira replied. "I swear, I never would've

done it if I thought they'd be in any danger."

"So you didn't do the food thing, but you did take the sets," Sasha prompted her.

"Yeah. And the ticket issues were me too."

"What for?" Cloe demanded.

"So first, since I'd seen how much money you guys were raising for the environment, I figured the more tickets you sold, the better," Mira explained. "So I had a computer hacker friend rig the system so we could oversell. I didn't think about the amphitheatre's capacity limits, but I thought it was awesome how you guys did two concerts back to back."

"It wasn't so awesome when we were dragging ourselves off the stage at the end of the night," Jade pointed out.

"Look, I'm sorry," Mira said. "I admit it, I didn't think it through. So then I decided it was time for me to start taking real action. I

110

organized 'Go Green day', and we planted all those trees in the morning, and kept right on doing service projects all day."

"But why undersell our tickets?" Sasha asked.

"I wanted as many people as possible to be involved in my volunteer day, so I thought if they couldn't get into your concert, they'd help out on our projects instead," Mira replied. "But I am glad you got people out there anyway – it turns out there are enough people who care about the environment to fill an amphitheatre *and* man a bunch of important projects."

"Okay, I think I get where you were coming from," Yasmin began, "but my question is, why didn't you just talk to us about all this in the first place? You could've helped us plan the whole thing from the beginning, and then there wouldn't have been any reason for all this competition."

"You girls have never spoken to me in school!" Mira exclaimed. "You didn't even recognize me backstage. I was surprised you even knew my name tonight."

"But if you felt this strongly about our tour, you should've pushed past your shyness or whatever and just talked to us," Sasha told her.

"Hold it. I didn't get to be Earth Club President by being *shy*," Mira retorted. "But you have to admit, you girls are kind of intimidating. I mean, you're these big-time pop stars, and I'm just... I'm just someone who wants to save the earth."

"But that's the thing!" Yasmin cried. "We're just ordinary girls trying to help out the planet, too. And I'm sorry if we came off as unapproachable, because that's totally not who we are."

"I see that now, and I'm really sorry for all

112

the trouble I caused," Mira said quietly. "I'm just glad that, despite all of my mistakes, the tour has still been a huge success. You girls really have made a difference, and I'm utterly impressed."

"Well, thanks," Sasha replied.

"Hey, girls, I think I have an idea for how we can make all of this right," Yasmin interrupted, and the others all turned to her to listen to her plan.

Chapter 12

Mira rode in the Lucky Starz' tour van on the drive to Washington, D.C., and they spent the whole drive discussing how to make the most of the final leg of their tour.

When they rolled into the nation's capital, the girls, along with the other bands, spent the evening planning for their meeting the next day with the Congressional committee on the environment. They would all sit in on the meeting, but they decided that they would divide the speaking between Mira for her knowledge, Yasmin for her passion and Sasha for her public-speaking skills.

"Together, we'll be an invincible team!" Yasmin declared.

The girls spoke at the Congressional

hearing, and the senators and representatives all seemed totally impressed. They promised they would take the girls' suggestions for helping the environment into consideration.

"Do you think they really will?" Mira asked worriedly as they left the capital building.

"Hey, if anyone could convince them, it was you girls!" Jade reassured her.

Next they headed to a stream clean-up, where they cleared out rubbish, replanted trees and weeded out invasive plants, with the help of Mira's band of volunteers, along with lots of local Earth Club members she had rallied for the cause.

This time, instead of spending most of the event talking to the press like they had at the ocean clean-up, or ducking out early for their concert like they had at the desert landscaping event, the band members worked straight through until the absolute last second.

There were still camera crews and interviewers there, and the band members were willing to answer questions, but they didn't let the press interfere with their work for more than a few minutes at a time.

"That was *way* more satisfying that spending the whole time giving on-air sound bites!" Cloe declared afterward. "Mira, you really do know your way around a volunteer event!"

"That's pretty much what I spend all of my time doing," Mira explained. "So I'd better be good at it by now!"

That night, Mira ran the festival booths, along with a group of her volunteer pals. With their understanding of the issues and enthusiasm for pitching in, the new volunteers got the concert-goers so excited about the topics at each of their booths that the seats in the auditorium were never completely full – people were constantly circulating around the displays, and instead of just signing up for mailing lists and service events, they were asking questions about how to help and coming up with ideas for events they could organize themselves.

This was exactly what Yasmin had envisioned for the festival, but hadn't known how to execute on her own. Now, as she wandered through the crowd while the other bands performed, she only wished that Mira had joined their team weeks ago. Yasmin just knew that they would have had a much

bigger impact with the benefit of Mira's expert advice.

Yasmin was so entranced by the excitement and energy amongst the concert-goers that she almost forgot to go backstage in time for her own band's set. But then she heard The Tiger Stripes singing their song "Save the World", and she realized it was almost time for her to go on.

Now that the bands had been travelling and performing together constantly for almost two weeks, they were totally in tune with each other, and the show flowed so well that the band members all admitted to each other backstage that they didn't know how they could ever perform separately again.

After the "Charmed Planet" finale number, Yasmin grabbed the microphone and announced, "There's someone we'd like to introduce you to, who's out there helping the

Earth each and every day. Mira Iyer, come up here!"

A huge spotlight searched the crowd, and zoned in on Mira, making her way through the crowd. When she stepped onto the stage, all the band members ran over to her, surrounding her in a massive group hug.

"We're so grateful to all of you for coming out and supporting this tour, and we couldn't imagine a better place to finish it than in our nation's capital!" Sasha added, and the audience erupted in cheers.

"But now that the tour is coming to an end, let's all try to be more like Mira, and make a difference in our everyday lives, not just at big events like this," Sasha continued, drawing more applause from the crowd.

Mira looked embarrassed, but the others pushed her forward and she nervously took a bow. The crowd gave them all a standing

ovation as they rushed off the stage.

"I can't believe you did that!" Mira gasped backstage.

"I'm sorry, I just thought–" Yasmin began.

"No, it was fantastic!" Mira interrupted. "I mean, you guys told an entire auditorium of people to be more like me – that's got to be the best compliment ever!"

"Are you free for our wrap party tonight?" Jade asked. "It'll just be all of us bands, but we'd love to have you there."

"That sounds great," Mira agreed. "And hey, do you think you could introduce me to that cute bass player from The Tiger Stripes – it's Parker, right?"

"Did I hear my name?" Parker inquired, coming up behind the girls. "Hi Mira. It's an honour to meet you."

Mira blushed, but Parker was so friendly

that she soon felt totally at ease. Mira rode back to the hotel in The Tiger Stripes' van, while Tristan and Cody rode in the Lucky Starz' van to hang out with Yasmin and Cloe.

They all gathered in the hotel's restaurant, which had stayed open late so the bands could have dinner after their show. They talked and ate and laughed until late into the night, making plans for volunteer projects back in their hometowns and a reunion tour the next summer.

By the time they said goodnight to Mira and headed back to their suite, Cloe, Jade, Sasha and Yasmin were also the newest members of the Stilesville High Earth Club. They were thrilled with the attention they had received for issues facing the environment throughout their tour, but they were excited to be a part of a local, ongoing, hands-on effort as well.

When the four best friends reached their suite, they stayed up even later, giggling and talking about their new crushes – Cody, Brady, Carter and Tristan.

"I'm so glad we got to meet such cool guys on this tour!" Cloe exclaimed.

"I know – I hope we really do a reunion tour so we can see them again," Sasha added. When her friends gave her knowing grins, she insisted, "Because they're really good musicians! That's all!"

"Right," Jade teased. "You're just impressed by Carter's guitar skills."

"What?" Sasha protested. "I am! Anyway, The Tiger Stripes are in Seattle, and The Dragons are in LA, so it shouldn't be *too* hard for us to meet up with them again."

"True," Jade agreed. "And we *are* on the same record label, after all."

"You know who I'm glad we met?" Yasmin interrupted. "Mira. She's a great girl, and I can't believe we've been going to school with her all this time and didn't know her at all."

"She *did* almost ruin our tour, though," Cloe pointed out.

"No, she didn't," Yasmin replied. "She didn't throw anything at us that we couldn't handle."

"Well, of course not!" Jade exclaimed. "Because together, we can handle anything!"

"Even saving the planet!" Yasmin declared, and her best friends all agreed.

©MGA

Read more about Bratz in these other awesome books!

BRATZ™